Contents

1 You're Fired! 1

2 The Cattle Were Gone! 5

3 Plans for Tornado 9

4 Fawn — A New Friend 13

5 The Art of Horse-Breaking 17

6 The Race Horse 20

7 Western Weekend 26

8 Getting Even 34

9 Over the Cliff 39

Chapter 1

You're Fired!

Jack walked up the road to the Flying Y ranch house. He was carrying his saddle and was tired. He had asked for work at every ranch along the way. The answer was always, "Sorry, no riders needed."

The young cowhand stopped at a small corral. There a bronco was being saddled for the first time. One man held the bridle and twisted the horse's ear. This was done to distract the horse while the other man mounted.

For a moment the red horse stood there shaking. He was surprised by the man's weight on his back. His large black eyes looked terrified. His ears moved back and forth. Other cowboys stood outside the corral. They watched to see what might happen.

Suddenly a tumbleweed blew into the corral. It bounced and rolled as if it were alive. The horse jumped, nearly throwing his rider. The rider

Suddenly a tumbleweed blew into the corral. The horse jumped, nearly throwing his rider.

spurred him hard. The horse snorted in pain. Blood oozed from the cuts on his sides. Again, the spurs. The horse bucked, trying to rid himself of his cruel rider. He reared and fell over. The heavy saddle was smashed. The rider had jumped off just in time.

"Tornado's got a mean streak," the rider said. He was a horse-breaker for the ranch.

"You're the one who's mean, Zeke," Clay, the foreman, said. He had been watching Zeke ride the horse. "You scared that young horse. Now he'll be dangerous. That's the last Flying Y horse you'll ruin. You're fired!"

Zeke looked at Clay. His face twisted into an ugly sneer. He knew there was no use talking. He turned away. He was mad. "I'll get even!"

Clay's face was red with anger. He walked to the frightened horse. He put his hand on the shaking animal to calm him. But Tornado laid back his ears and tried to bite. The old cattleman slapped his nose. But he spoke without anger. "You're just scared, aren't you, Tornado?" He took off the broken saddle. Shaking his head sadly, he led the red horse from the corral.

"Fear makes a horse dangerous," Clay said as he handed the reins to a cowhand. "We don't have time to spend with a spoiled horse. Tornado's a total loss to the ranch."

Seeing how angry the foreman was, Jack started to walk away. This was no time to ask for work. But the foreman called, "What do you want?"

"A job," replied Jack.

"I don't need another rider," said the foreman. He looked at Jack's saddle.

"What about the horse-breaker's job?" Jack asked. Maybe there was a chance.

"I made one mistake by hiring Zeke. I'm not hiring another young fellow with no experience." Then he added, "Well, if you need a job, you can fix fences. And, by the way, my name's Clay."

No riding. No cattle. No friends. Just long days of fixing broken wire. But it was a job. "OK," said Jack. "Thanks."

"Don't thank me," the foreman said. "Just do a good job. The bunkhouse is over there." He pointed to a low brown building. "You can drop your gear off there."

Jack picked up his saddle and his bag and walked to the bunkhouse. Inside it was plain but clean. Jack laid down on one of the empty bunks. It was good to have a job — and he would be near horses.

Chapter 2

The Cattle Were Gone!

The next morning Jack had pancakes and bacon for breakfast. Then he went to work. He loaded the pickup truck with rolls of wire. Then he drove along miles of fences that went along the Flying Y. He looked for a broken part of the fence. Then he would fix it. The prairie was purple and green. It stretched flat as a table to the base of the Teton Mountains. The ranch was near Jackson, Wyoming. It was beautiful country. Jack worked hard, cutting away rusty wire and fixing fences. But he kept wishing that he could be working with horses and cattle.

One spring evening a cowhand named Curly said to Jack, "I'll need you tomorrow. You can put your saddle on old Sal. She's a little lame but strong enough for this job. We'll go up the mountain and round up strays."

It was raining the next morning. Jack went out

to saddle Sal. He put beef jerky, biscuits, and bacon into his saddle bags. Then he rolled up his blankets. He tied them to the back of his saddle. Jack didn't mind the rain. He was happy to be doing a cowhand's job.

The sure-footed stock horses moved up the rocky trail. They came to a high meadow. Curly said, "The stray cattle will probably be around here. The grass is good."

They got off their horses and tied them to the trees. Then they ate some beef jerky. Later on they cut down some small trees and built a small corral.

"That will hold the strays tonight," Curly said.

The rest of the day Curly and Jack looked for cattle. They found six cows with newborn calves and drove them into the corral.

"You stay here tonight with them," Curly told Jack. "I'll go back down to the ranch. I want to help the vet in the morning when he gives the cattle their shots. When I'm finished, I'll come back here. Then we'll drive the strays down to the ranch. Stay near the cattle. Don't leave them."

So Jack stayed alone on the mountain. He tied Sal's front feet together so she couldn't run away. The rain stopped. It was cold at 7,000 feet above sea level. Jack found a safe place to build a fire.

He cleared a ten-foot circle, brushing away pine needles and loose branches. When he got down to soil that wouldn't burn, he built a fire. Then he fried some bacon.

It was getting dark. A mountain lion screamed in the distance. The cattle began to move. They knew there was a killer nearby. Jack got his harmonica out and played it awhile to quiet the cattle. Then he rolled up in his blankets. The sky was full of bright stars. He dozed off.

Twigs crackled. Jack sat up and reached for his rifle. Was it the mountain lion?

"Hey there, don't shoot!" said a voice in the dark. "Help me, will yuh? My car stopped on the old logging road. I was taking my wife to the hospital. She's sick."

"What can I do?" asked Jack. He could see the outline of a man in the darkness.

"Ride down to the Flying Y and come back with a pickup," the stranger said. When Jack didn't answer, he pleaded, "Please. My wife's really sick."

Jack looked at the stray cattle. "I can't leave 'em," he said.

"I'll guard 'em. I've been ranching for years. You ride down and get help. Hurry!"

Jack decided to help the stranger. He put the

saddle on Sal and started down the trail. The mountain lion screamed. Jack didn't feel good about all of this. Was he doing the right thing?

When he got to the ranch, he put Sal in the pasture. He got the pickup and drove up the rocky logging road. But when he got near his camp, there was no stalled car or sick woman.

Jack didn't know what to do. He jumped out and ran through the woods to the corral. The cattle were gone! The gate was open. Only human hands could open that gate. The cattle had been stolen! Jack could hear Curly telling him, "Don't leave 'em."

Jack went back to the ranch. He told Clay what had happened. "You were told not to leave 'em," Clay shouted. "You're a total loss as a cowhand. You'd better stick to fixing fences."

Later Curly told Jack that cattle rustlers were known to be in the Jackson area. They were experts at quickly trucking away cattle. The Flying Y strays were probably many miles away by now.

Jack really wanted to pay the ranch for those lost strays. He tried to think of ways to get some money. That evening he saw the red bronco in the pasture. He thought of Clay's words, "Tornado's a total loss to the ranch." Tornado and Jack, he thought, were both complete losses.

That night Jack had a dream.

Chapter 3

Plans for Tornado

In his dream Jack was riding a red stock horse. It was a horse trained to herd cattle. It raced along beside a runaway steer. Jack threw a lasso over the steer's horns. He tied the other end of the rope to the saddle horn. Then he reined in Tornado to a stop. He jerked the steer off its feet. Then he jumped off and ran to the steer. Tornado kept the rope tight to stop the steer from getting up. Jack quickly tied the steer's legs together. This would help it to lie still while it was being branded.

Then he woke up. What a wonderful dream he had had. Why not train Tornado to be a top stock horse? Then he could pay the Flying Y for the loss of the cattle!

Suddenly Jack remembered how Tornado had reared and crashed over. What if Tornado did that while Jack was training him? Would Jack be quick enough to save himself? A cold sweat broke out on his skin. He was afraid. But he still wanted to try to train Tornado.

Jack got out of bed. He was careful not to wake up the other cowhands. He got his saddle from the barn. Then he walked out into the pasture under the dark sky. Tornado saw him and ran away. Jack went back to the barn and filled a bucket with oats. He whistled and shook the bucket so that the oats made a noise. Tornado listened. His ears moved forward. His nose shook. He wanted those oats. He quietly came to Jack. Then he put his muzzle into the oats and ate. Jack tossed a rope over Tornado's neck and tied him to the fence post. Next he saddled and bridled him. Then he untied Tornado and quietly mounted. When Tornado felt Jack's weight on his back, he bucked and reared. Jack hit the ground hard. Tornado ran to the other end of the pasture. It took Jack an hour to get close enough to Tornado to take off the saddle.

Being able to ride Tornado was just a dream, Jack thought. Tornado will never be a stock horse. He's a complete loss to the ranch.

The rest of the day Jack worked hard. But he couldn't get Tornado out of his mind. Tornado was such a fine horse. It was sad to think he might be useless for the rest of his life. There has to be a way, he thought.

The next day Curly asked Jack to help shoe some of the horses. Jack was to catch one horse at a time. Then he would bring the horse to the shoer whose name was Jose. Jose would replace loose and outgrown horseshoes.

The horses were afraid of the fire in the little stove on Jose's pickup truck. They were afraid of the sparks that flew from Jose's iron anvil. He pounded the heated steel shoes into shape to fit each horse. The horses were afraid when he pounded nails into their hooves, even though it didn't hurt. Jose worked every day with horses that were afraid.

"I need your help, Jose," Jack said. "I want to train a horse that is afraid of a rider." He told Jose about how Tornado was ruined by Zeke.

"Why do you want to train a bad horse like that?" Jose asked.

Jack told him that he wanted to repay the ranch for the lost cattle. He could do this by training a good stock horse.

"But Tornado is a wild horse, Jack," said Jose. He dropped a red-hot horseshoe into a bucket of cold water. The hot steel hissed in the water. "You need help from someone who knows how

11

to train wild horses," Jose added.

"Who?" asked Jack.

"Indians," answered Jose. "They catch mustangs in the mountains. They know how to tame wild horses. You go to the reservation and ask for Fawn. Maybe she will help you."

Chapter 4

Fawn—A New Friend

The following Sunday Jack put on new jeans and a blue shirt and cleaned his boots. He rode Sal to the nearby Indian reservation. Then he asked for Fawn at the grocery store. The grocer said she lived at her father's ranch in the hills.

Jack started up the mountain road. Soon he met an Indian girl riding bareback on a pinto horse.

"Pretty horse," Jack said to the girl.

"Thanks," the girl said, not stopping.

Jack turned Sal down the mountain road again. He wanted to ride next to the girl.

"Are you Fawn?" he asked.

She gave a little nod. He said, "Would you talk to me about my horse?"

For the first time Fawn looked at him. Then she bent and patted the old mare. "What's the matter?" she asked.

For the first time, Fawn looked at him. Then she bent and patted the old mare.

Jack told Fawn all about Tornado. Then he said, "The horse shoer said that you would tell me how to tame a wild horse."

"No, I won't," Fawn said.

Jack was surprised. "Why not?" he asked.

"Because telling is not enough. It takes time — much time."

"Can you do it?"

"Yes," said the Indian girl.

If she understands, maybe she'll help, Jack thought. He told her how Zeke had ruined Tornado's trust in people. He told her about the stolen cattle. Finally he told her that he wanted to tame Tornado and train him to be a top stock horse. This way he could repay the ranch for the lost cattle.

Fawn stopped her pinto horse. She looked at Jack again and said, "Can you build a barn?"

"Sure," said Jack in surprise.

"Then I'll help you tame your wild horse. But you must help me build a barn. The winter is cold. My horses need shelter from the snow."

"I could come on Sundays," Jack said. He wondered what he was getting himself into. But he liked the idea of spending Sundays with Fawn. She had large brown eyes and beautiful black hair. And she had a quiet way of walking and talking. Her name fit her.

Fawn and Jack rode to the Flying Y together. Clay saw them coming in the gate. He walked to the hitching rail to greet Fawn. Jack was surprised that Clay knew her.

"Fawn was the rodeo queen at Western Weekend last summer," Clay said. "She's a good hand with a horse."

Jack saw his chance. "Fawn said she'd help me tame Tornado," he said.

Clay frowned. He didn't think much of Jack since the cattle were stolen.

"That so, Fawn?" Clay asked.

"I can tame Tornado the Indian way," Fawn answered quietly.

"But that's going to take a lot of work, Fawn," Clay told her.

"Jack will repay me," she said.

Clay looked at them. He knew Tornado was worthless. Why would Jack want to train a dangerous horse? Then he thought about Fawn's word "repay." "You want to train Tornado to repay the ranch for the stolen cattle?" Clay asked.

"Yeah," said Jack. He was glad that Clay understood.

Clay turned towards the corral. Then he stopped and smiled back at Fawn and Jack. "All right, go ahead and try it," he said.

As Jack fixed fences during the next week, he thought about Fawn. He thought about how straight she sat on War Paint, her pinto horse. He thought about how quietly she spoke. He thought of how her long braids moved as she walked. He liked the way her brown arms looked with their silver and blue bracelets.

Chapter 5

The Art of Horse-Breaking

On Sunday Fawn arrived at the Flying Y at dawn. She drove a truck carrying sacks, tin cans, ropes, and blankets. "Today we'll begin to tame him," she told Jack. Then she jumped down from the truck.

Fawn pushed her braids up under her cowboy hat. She rolled up her sleeves and tucked her shirt into her jeans. On her silver belt buckle were the words "Rodeo Queen, Western Weekend." She was ready for the hard work ahead.

Fawn wouldn't let Jack trap Tornado with oats. She and Jack walked into the pasture. They went up over a hill to where the horses grazed. Fawn did not enter the herd. Instead, she started to circle around it from a distance. The horses would get used to her and Jack and would not run away. Jack felt that what Fawn was doing would take forever. But then he thought about

17

how long it had taken him to get close enough to Tornado to even get the saddle off.

Fawn walked quietly. Sometimes she stopped and gave a soft whistle. The horses raised their heads and looked at her. Fawn and Jack stood still. When the horses didn't see anything to fear, they went back to grazing. Fawn and Jack continued their slow walk around the herd. They stopped now and then to whistle. Each time they walked around the herd, their circle became smaller. They were soon close to the herd. All the horses could see them. But they were not scared. They did not suddenly turn and run away. Fawn walked into the herd. She went to Tornado and put her rope over his neck. Then she put a halter on him and led him out of the pasture.

"See?" she said. "We didn't need oats to catch Tornado."

Fawn led Tornado down the road to the small corral. This corral was used just for breaking horses. Then she led the horse inside to a strong wooden post. She tied the halter rope to the post. Next she tied another rope around Tornado's neck with a bowline knot. Then she tied this to a rope that held one of Tornado's hooves up off the ground. Now he couldn't kick her.

Tornado's taming was about to start. Fawn

went to the pickup and took out a tumbleweed.

"What are you going to do?" Jack asked.

"A tumbleweed started all the trouble. I'm going to teach Tornado not to be afraid of things that blow in his way," Fawn told Jack. She began to pet the horse gently with the little bush.

Tornado didn't like it. He pulled back, trying to break his halter rope. Then he tried to kick Fawn, but he couldn't because one hind hoof was tied up, and he needed the other to stand on. Fawn rubbed the bush gently all over Tornado, down his legs and under his belly. Little by little the horse began to understand that the bush wasn't hurting him. When he finally stood still, Fawn knew he had learned his lesson. She offered Tornado the tumbleweed. He nibbled it. Fawn and Jack laughed.

Chapter 6

The Race Horse

Fawn asked Jack to put his saddle on Tornado. She went to her pickup and brought back two sacks filled with empty cans. They made a noise when Fawn shook them. She tied one on each side of Tornado's saddle. Then she untied the ropes and set Tornado free in the corral. The sacks bumped his sides. The cans made a lot of noise. Tornado was scared. He bucked, trying to get rid of the noisy sacks. The more he bucked, the more they banged and clanged. He galloped around and around. The sacks were swinging at his sides. Slowly he knew that he wasn't being hurt. Finally he came to a stop.

"He's tired. Now's your chance," said Fawn. "He'll like you better than the cans." She put a bridle on Tornado and held him while Jack took off the sacks. Then Jack swung up into the saddle. Tornado moved his ears back. Somebody was on him! But he didn't buck. He waited to see what would happen.

Fawn said softly, "Come on, Tornado," and led him forward. The tired horse followed her a few steps. Fawn stopped. "That's enough for to-day," she said.

Jack had to fix fences every day the next week. But when he was finished, he went out to the pasture. He caught Tornado the way Fawn had showed him. Then he tied Tornado to the post in the corral and tied one leg up. He patted the horse with sacks, soft blankets, and tumble-weeds. Tornado hated this "sacking out," but each day he was less scared.

Jack tied the two sacks full of empty cans onto Tornado's saddle. Then he turned the horse loose in the corral. Tornado galloped and bucked. It did no good. The sacks still rode him. By the end of the week Tornado stopped bucking.

The following Sunday Jack showed Fawn that Tornado was becoming gentle.

"We'll add some new lessons," she said. Again they tied Tornado to the post and tied up his leg. Fawn took a metal washtub from her truck. She put it next to the horse. Then she began to throw empty cans into it. Tornado was scared by the noise. He pulled back, trying to break his halter rope and get away. "Do this every day, and soon loud noises won't scare him," Fawn said. "Give him this lesson in the evening. Then you can give him his oats in the washtub. He'll learn not to be afraid of it."

Each Sunday Fawn added new lessons. She taught the horse to stand quietly with a sack around his front feet. She taught him to pull a rubber tire on the end of a rope tied to his saddle horn. Tornado learned to stand quietly while Jack climbed on and off him. Jack repeated the lessons each evening after he had fixed fences all day.

One Sunday Fawn told Jack, "He's getting gentle. Now you can start riding him. But no spurs. Next Sunday you come to my father's ranch and help build the barn."

Each evening Jack rode Tornado around and around the corral. He taught the horse to turn. He would pull the rein the way he wanted to go. Then he would slap the other side of the horse's neck. Tornado learned fast, but it was only a start. It would take years to teach Tornado all the things a top stock horse should know. But Tornado had already learned the best lesson: trust.

The next Sunday Jack saddled Tornado. "We're going to visit Fawn," he told the horse.

When Tornado saw the open road in front of him, he seemed happy. He didn't try to throw Jack. Soon they arrived at Fawn's father's ranch. Jack tied Tornado with the sack and let him graze.

"We've got some help," said Fawn with a laugh. Jack was surprised to see a dozen Indians sawing and nailing up the frame of a barn.

"I thought that was my job," Jack said.

"You can help," said Fawn. She had wanted to see how much work Jack was willing to do to repay her. Jack met her brothers, uncles, cousins, and neighbors. "This is the way we used to put up a barn," she said. "We'll have it up by dinner. Then we'll have Mama's stew."

Jack worked hard carrying lumber, sawing, and nailing. By sundown they were finished with the barn roof. Fawn's mother brought out her stew. There were also ears of corn, fresh baked bread, and green vegetables from her garden. They sat down at long tables her brothers had made.

Finally it was time for Jack to say good night to Fawn. "I was hoping that the barn would take a lot longer to build," he told her.

The girl smiled and said, "Would you like to come again? You can help me halter-break some young horses for the sale at Western Weekend."

"I'll be here next Sunday," Jack said happily.

During the next week Jack rode Tornado in the evenings. They liked going out across the prairie. Tornado jumped back from jack rabbits and deer that jumped out of the bushes. But he didn't try to throw Jack.

One Sunday morning on the way to Fawn's ranch, Tornado wanted to gallop. "Oh, no," laughed Jack. "Now you think you're a race horse."

A race horse. A race horse. The words beat in Jack's brain as Tornado's hoofs beat on the road. Could Tornado be a race horse? It would be years before Tornado could learn to be a top stock horse. But he could be a race horse *now*. Horses racing in the Kentucky Derby are three-year-olds. That was Tornado's age now!

Jack came to the last mile before the reservation. Here there were no big rocks or holes in the road. Finally he let Tornado gallop. All of a sudden, the horse seemed happy. His hooves beat faster and faster. The wind whistled past Jack's ears. "You're flying, boy. Flying," Jack told the red horse.

Soon they arrived at Fawn's father's ranch. Fawn looked at the tired horse. "Did he run away with you?" she asked Jack.

"No. I wanted to see how fast he is. We galloped the last mile. Maybe he could be a race horse" Jack said.

A race horse. A race horse. Now the words were going around in Fawn's head. She and Jack walked toward the pasture. Maybe the horse that had been a total loss would become a race horse now! Fawn turned to Jack and said, "Soon there will be a three-day race at Western Weekend in Jackson. Could you get Tornado ready by then?"

Chapter 7

Western Weekend

Fawn and Jack talked as they trained her yearlings. "There's a prize for the winner of the Western Weekend race," Fawn said. She pulled on the halter of a colt. "The prize is a thousand dollars!"

A thousand dollars! Enough to repay the ranch for the cattle, thought Jack.

"How can I get Tornado ready for the race?" Jack asked.

"Climbing up hills is the best way," said Fawn. "It makes strong muscles. But it doesn't hurt the legs because there is no hard galloping."

After that, each morning and evening Jack rode Tornado up the logging road. At first it was hard for the horse. But every day it became a little easier. And every day he could go a little farther.

One morning after his ride, Jack met up with Clay.

"You're doing a good job with Tornado," the old man said.

Now's my chance, thought Jack. He asked Clay if he could race Tornado at Western Weekend.

"The best horses in Wyoming will be there," Clay said. He looked at Tornado's strong muscles.

"There just can't be a horse better than Tornado," Jack said. "Let me race him for the Flying Y."

Clay knew that Jack had worked hard to tame that spoiled, dangerous horse. It could be a waste of time and money to try to race him. Yet, Clay and Jack were alike in one way—they both liked horses.

"All right," Clay said. "You can pull my horse trailer with the pickup. Good luck."

Finally the day for Western Weekend came. Fawn drove her cattle truck down to the Jackson fairgrounds. It was full of yearlings ready to be sold. Jack followed Fawn with Clay's horse trailer.

Jack unloaded Tornado. The horse looked good. His red coat shone, and he was fat from the extra oats Jack had been feeding him. But Tornado was scared by all the new things around him. He seemed jumpy as Jack led him to the stable.

Fawn drove up in her truck. She unloaded the yearlings and put each one in a stall. Then she and Jack had supper at the race track cafe.

Later Fawn and Jack came back to the stable and saddled Tornado. They wanted to take him for a quiet walk to get him used to the track. Fawn rode War Paint and led Tornado with Jack on his back. They didn't want Tornado to think he was going for a gallop. They stopped at the metal starting gate that stretched across the track. Tornado smelled it and touched it with his muzzle. Fawn spoke to the horse. She helped him learn that this gate wasn't going to hurt him.

The Western Weekend lasted for three days. If the same horse won on both the first and second days, the thousand dollar prize went to him. But sometimes two horses each won a race. Then just those two alone raced for the cash prize on the third day.

The morning of the first race, Jack saddled Tornado at dawn. They went out for a slow run on the track. Jack wanted to exercise the horse before the race. At home Tornado was free in a large pasture, but at the racetrack he had to stay in a stall. When he saw the long track in front of him, Tornado became excited. Jack tried to quiet him, "It's just like the road to Fawn's father's ranch, boy. Now be quiet and walk." But Tornado saw the other race horses out there, too. He wanted to run with them.

Suddenly, Tornado started to run away with Jack. He was moving fast. The track rushed by. Jack pulled on the reins. He tried to stop the horse. Tornado galloped faster and faster. Behind them a black horse was running to get ahead of Tornado. Soon the two horses were running together. They came around the turn. The black horse forced Tornado away from the rail. He was bigger, older, stronger.

Jack knew he had to stop Tornado. The horse would be worn out before the afternoon race. Jack stood in his stirrups and jerked the reins. Tornado shook his head. Hadn't they come to race?

There were a lot of people at the track that morning. They had seen Tornado's quick run. Most of them would bet that afternoon. Some had stop watches. A fat man shouted, "Want to sell that red horse, son?"

Jack just smiled and shook his head. But as he walked the tired horse past the crowd, Jack worried. Had the run been too hard on the young horse?

"Too fast. Too fast," Fawn said. She pulled the lead rope on Tornado.

"He's young and strong. It's only a quarter-of-a-mile race," Jack said. But he knew that Tornado might already have lost that race.

By 1:00 p.m. the stands were full. Jack wore a bright blue racing shirt and cap. He carried his light racing saddle. Before he could race, Tornado had to be weighed. Fawn, on War Paint, led Tornado to the paddock. There they would wait for the bugle call for the race.

The black horse was already there. He walked quietly behind his groom. This older horse had been to the races before. He knew he would soon have his chance on the track. Six other horses were there from the biggest ranches in Wyoming. They all walked behind their grooms in the circle.

Clay came to the paddock and saddled Tornado. Then he helped Jack mount. Nobody said anything. Everyone was too excited.

Then the bugle called the horses to the starting gate. They walked single file past the stands. Then the announcer said over the public address system, "Ladies and gentlemen, the first race of the Western Weekend three-day race is about to be run."

The starting bell rang. The gate opened. The horses ran out. In seconds the black was in the lead. A grey was second. Tornado was third.

Jack hit Tornado with the whip. Those long climbs in the mountains had hardened his muscles. Tornado was young. His legs were strong. Now he was able to start moving up to the front. He ran past the grey. Jack sat over Tornado's neck. He felt Tornado's hooves going faster and faster. He heard Tornado's breath coming in short gasps. He smelled the horse's sweat. Tornado was giving all the speed he had. "Good boy!" Jack said.

Tornado's nose almost reached the black's flying tail. He was gaining on the leader. But too late! They dashed past the finish line, the black first, Tornado second.

Both riders stood up in their stirrups and pulled back on the reins. They were trying to slow their horses. Tornado still wanted to race. "There's still tomorrow, boy," Jack said.

Fawn rode War Paint up beside Tornado. She put a rope on his bridle. "Tomorrow will be better when Tornado's more rested," she said and smiled. She and Jack rode their horses past the crowd. Suddenly Jack saw the cruel horsebreaker he'd seen that first day at the Flying Y. Zeke was smiling as he counted his money. He had bet on the black horse and won.

Jack saddled Tornado before dawn on the

morning of the second day's race. He put a flashlight in his pocket. Then he rode out to the track in the dark. No other horses were there yet. Jack made Tornado gallop slowly over the quarter-mile course. He wanted to show the horse how far to go and where the race ended.

Soon it was 1:00 p.m. Jack and Tornado were in the starting gate once more. Jack was scared. It's now or never, he thought. If we don't win this one, we've lost the thousand dollars.

The bell rang. The gate opened. The horses ran out. In a few seconds Tornado was in the lead. Jack felt his strong horse under him. Nothing could stop Tornado now. The black horse was coming up fast on the inside rail. Never mind, thought Jack. Tornado is going to win.

Then Jack saw it. A piece of white paper was blowing across the track, right in the way of Tornado. What would he do?

The galloping red horse also saw the paper. His ears moved. He was listening to the sounds of the black horse coming up behind him. Tornado ran even faster. He galloped straight and fast, right over the blowing paper.

Tornado and the black got across the finish line. At that moment the announcer shouted, "Tornado of the Flying Y is first!" Now there

The galloping red horse also saw the paper. His ears moved and he galloped right over the paper.

would be a third race. It would be the most exciting race of all. The thousand dollars would belong to the winner.

Chapter 8

Getting Even

That night Zeke counted his money. He had bet his first day's winnings on the black horse in the second race. This time he had lost. He was very mad. He took some weeds out of a paper bag. "Tomorrow I'll make sure the black horse wins," he said to himself. He chopped up the loco weed and mixed it into some oats. "This will make Tornado forget about racing. I told them I'd get even with the Flying Y." Tomorrow he'd bet on the black and win.

Fawn and Jack got to the stable early the next morning. Jack saddled Tornado and took him onto the track for a slow gallop. War Paint galloped next to him. By this time Tornado knew his job — a short, easy gallop in the morning, but flying speed in the afternoon race. He galloped easily next to War Paint. After Jack slowed down from the gallop, he still pranced.

Fawn snapped the lead rope onto Tornado's bridle. She led him back to the stable. Jack was still on his back. Then Jack jumped down and unsaddled the tired horse. He poured a bucket of warm water over Tornado's back. Then he rubbed it off. Next he put a blanket over Tornado. He led him slowly round and round. He did this to quiet the horse down. Fawn cleaned the stall and the saddle and bridle. She made sure everything was ready for the race. Then she and Jack went to the cafe for breakfast.

Zeke was at the track early, too, that morning. He saw Fawn and Jack leave the stable. He went to his old car and took out the bag of loco weed and oats. Then he put this inside his coat. He slowly walked down the row of stalls. He stopped when he came to Tornado. Thinking no one was watching, he dumped the mixture into Tornado's feed bucket. As he walked away, he passed the Flying Y's pickup truck. Jack had left the keys inside. This was done in case a horse van driver needed to move it in order to get by.

Just before the 1:00 p.m. race, Zeke bet the last of his money on the black horse. Then he waited at the rail near the finish line for the race to begin.

Back at the stable Fawn looked at Tornado.

Thinking no one was watching, he dumped the mixture into Tornado's feed bucket.

"Tornado looks sleepy, Jack," she said.

Jack stared at Tornado. The horse was beginning to stagger around his stall. "He's been drugged," Jack said in a low, angry voice.

They called the track vet. She looked at Tornado. "Yes," he said, "He has been drugged! It's something like loco weed. He'll be sleepy today, but he'll be all right tomorrow. You'll have to take him out of the race."

Fawn and Jack sadly went to the race track office where the vet made her report. The race would have to be called off. While they were talking, the trainer of the black horse came in. "I hear your horse is sick. I saw a fellow hanging around his stall this morning. I know him. It was Zeke, the horse-breaker."

Maybe Zeke drugged Tornado, Jack thought. But why?

A few minutes later the people at the race heard the announcer say, "Ladies and gentlemen, the race has been called off. All bets are off. Save your tickets. You will get your money back."

Standing at the rail, Zeke got scared. They know that Tornado has been drugged, he thought. I wonder if anybody saw me! I've got to get away!

But Zeke's old car couldn't go very fast. Suddenly he thought of the car keys in the Flying Y pickup. He ran straight to the stable area. He walked up to the pickup as if it were his own. Then he got in and drove away.

Fawn and Jack returned to the stable. Then they discovered that the Flying Y's pickup was missing. Jack called the sheriff. The sheriff told him not to worry. There were only a few roads out of Jackson. His deputies would know a pickup with "Flying Y" painted on the door.

There was nothing for Jack to do but keep an eye on Tornado. The drug would wear off soon. Sitting on some hay, Jack thought about his bad luck. It all started with the stolen cattle. He thought of the man who came to his campfire to ask for help. Jack hadn't seen his face, but he had heard his voice. The voice! Suddenly Jack realized he had heard it before. It was the first day at the Flying Y. Jack had heard that voice muttering, "I'll get even." It was the voice of Zeke. Did Zeke steal the cattle? Jack wondered. Did Zeke drug Tornado? Did he steal the pickup to get away?

Jack jumped up and ran to the telephone. He called the sheriff.

"Zeke, huh? We've been wanting to talk to him about stealing cattle," said the sheriff."

Chapter 9

Over the Cliff

Zeke knew he couldn't get far in that pickup. Too many people knew it. He turned off the main road onto a shortcut, the logging road. That road was old and full of rocks and holes. A sharp rock punched a hole in his radiator. The water dripped out. When the radiator was dry, the engine overheated and stopped. Zeke jumped out and ran into the woods.

Back at the race track, Fawn helped Jack load Tornado into her truck. She drove carefully to the Flying Y. She was afraid the drugged horse might fall down inside the truck.

The next day Fawn's cousin heard the news about the stolen pickup. He told Fawn that on the way home from Western Weekend, he had seen the Flying Y's pickup. It was turning up the old logging road. Fawn telephoned the sheriff. He left right away to go up the logging road to see what he could find.

Three miles up the road, the sheriff saw the pickup. He called back to his office, "The Flying Y is the nearest ranch. Phone the foreman and ask him to get a posse together for tomorrow morning. We'll search the woods. We think the thief is Zeke."

When Clay got the message, he went out to see the cowhands. "The sheriff just called. He's going after Zeke for stealing the Flying Y's pickup. Jack thinks Zeke also drugged Tornado and stole our cattle. The sheriff needs all of you for a posse to go find Zeke."

At dawn all the cowhands saddled their horses in the corral. The horses were excited. Tornado was OK now. Jack put a saddle on him.

The men rode up the logging road to the pickup. The sheriff was waiting. He had brought his horse in his horse trailer. "Be careful," he said. "Zeke is dangerous." The sheriff told them to spread out but stay close enough so they could call to each other.

Jack rode into the woods. He could hear someone else nearby, but soon he became separated from the others. He was alone. He searched for hours. Toward noon he head a noise near a cliff. He looked over the edge of the cliff. There was something down there. It wasn't moving. It was a man!

Jack quickly got off Tornado and tied him to a tree. He tied his lasso to a large tree at the edge of the cliff. He threw the other end down. Jack stepped over the rope with one foot. He pulled it up between his legs. Then he wrapped it across his right hip and brought it around across his chest to his left shoulder. Next he brought it across his back and under his right arm. He held the loose end in his right hand.

Little by little Jack let out the rope as he backed down the steep cliff. He reached the man. It was Zeke! Suddenly Zeke grabbed Jack's foot and tried to throw him over the ledge. It was 100 feet down to the bottom of the cliff. Only Jack's hold on the rope saved him from falling over the edge.

Zeke swung his fist at Jack. Jack had to drop the rope to defend himself. Zeke's next blow knocked Jack out for a moment.

When Jack came to, he heard something above him. Zeke was climbing up Jack's rope. When he got to the top, he untied the rope and threw it at Jack. "There's your rope. Now I'll take your horse and get out of here."

Zeke untied Tornado and mounted him. Tor-

Zeke swung his fist at Jack. His next blow knocked Jack out for a moment.

nado hated Zeke. He could never forget how Zeke had treated him.

He's not going to steal my horse, too, Jack thought. He whistled. Tornado knew that whistle. He turned around and threw Zeke. Then he headed toward the whistle.

Below on the ledge, Jack made a loop in the rope. He threw it up—three, four, five times. He was trying to drop it over a little tree on the side of the cliff. On the sixth throw, the rope caught hold. But would the little tree hold his weight? Jack looked down into the ravine below. If he fell, it would mean certain death.

He decided to try the climb. Slowly he climbed up. Up. Up. Up. He tried not to put much weight on the rope. Would it hold? Up. Up. Up. He climbed quickly, trying not to think of falling. Finally he reached the top. He was very tired. Tornado was there. Jack picked up the ends of the reins and mounted the horse.

But what about Zeke? Jack rode Tornado into the woods. He found Zeke lying where Tornado had dumped him. Jack dismounted and tied Zeke's hands and feet. He shoved Zeke over Tornado's saddle. Tornado jumped. He hated Zeke. Jack took the reins and led Tornado to the logging road. He walked for nearly an hour. By then, Zeke began to move.

Finally Jack saw the sheriff's car. The sheriff was talking over his radio.

"Hello! Hello!" shouted Jack. "I've got him!" The sheriff was happy that Zeke had been caught. He helped Jack get Zeke off Tornado and put him in the back of the patrol car. Then he fired two shots to call in the posse.

As the cowhands rode in, they all talked to Jack. He told them about the cliff and the fight with Zeke. Then he told them about climbing back up the cliff. The cowhands loved hearing what Tornado did when he heard Jack's whistle. Clay didn't say anything. He just listened.

The sheriff took Zeke. He was booked for cattle rustling, horse drugging, and car theft. Clay and Jack went in the car with the sheriff and Zeke. The cowhands led their horses back to the Flying Y.

"Well, Jack," Clay said as they drove along. "You did a good job training Tornado. I understand he'll come when you whistle now." Then he laughed. Zeke sank lower in his seat.

"I have some more young horses to break," Clay said to Jack. "Do you want the job?"